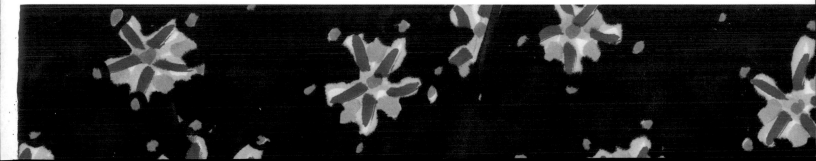

It was another September. All new classes, and a teacher I already knew I was going to love—my English teacher, Mr. Tranchina. He was funny and really cool! He woke something up in me. By the third week I was reading like a crazy person—more than I ever had—and writing, poems and stories and essays.

But then one day he asked us to read an essay on our families in front of the whole class.

MR. WAYNE'S
Masterpiece

Patricia Polacco

G. P. Putnam's Sons
An Imprint of Penguin Group (USA)

Patricia Lee Gauch, Editor

G. P. PUTNAM'S SONS
Published by the Penguin Group
Penguin Group (USA) LLC
375 Hudson Street, New York, NY 10014

USA | Canada | UK | Ireland | Australia | New Zealand | India | South Africa | China
penguin.com
A Penguin Random House Company

Library of Congress Cataloging-in-Publication Data
Polacco, Patricia.
Mr. Wayne's masterpiece / Patricia Polacco.
pages cm   Summary: Because she is afraid to read an essay aloud in English class,
young Patricia is invited to take Mr. Wayne's drama class where she paints sets,
participates in fun exercises, and memorizes every part in the play the others are
rehearsing. [1. Teachers—Fiction. 2. Theater—Fiction. 3. Schools—Fiction. 4. Public
speaking—Fiction.] I. Title. PZ7.P75186Mq 2014 [E]—dc23 2013046428
Manufactured in China by South China Printing Co. Ltd.
ISBN 978-0-399-16095-0
10 9 8 7 6 5 4 3 2 1

Design by Semadar Megged.   Text set in 14.5-point Adobe Devanagari.
The illustrations are rendered in pencils and markers.

*In loving memory of Thomas Wayne
and Joseph Tranchina*

y worst nightmare had come true when, after a few days of school, Mr. Tranchina asked me to read my essay out loud. I loved to write, but getting up and reading my essay in front of everybody? I just couldn't do it! No way. But when he called on me I had to do it.

I turned around, gripping the paper so tight that it fluttered like a bird in flight. My knees were knocking and my mouth was so dry I couldn't move my lower jaw. I was sure that the kids in the back could hear my heart beating.

I looked up. Everybody was looking at me. Everybody!

"Take a deep breath, dear," Mr. T. said softly from the front of the room. "Remember, everyone here is your friend. We really want to hear your essay."

But my voice wouldn't come out.

Finally Mr. T. let me go back to my seat. "It's all right, Patricia," he said.

I wanted to die.

Later that day Mr. T. said he had someone he wanted me to meet. It turned out to be Mr. Wayne, the drama teacher. The drama teacher!

"Mr. T. tells me that you are a crackerjack writer," Mr. Wayne said. He had the most wonderful smile.

"I like to write," I admitted.

"And he tells me that you have a problem getting up and speaking in front of the class." I just looked at the floor.

"Well, just maybe we can get you past that," he said, grinning and turning me toward a group of kids painting something on the floor. "Our class is working on a winter play."

My heart stopped in my chest. Drama Class! Winter play? Me? Was he kidding? Did he really think I could ever get up on a stage . . . in front of people? Maybe hundreds of people.

After supper Mom and I were sitting in our favorite chair together. She was a teacher now, but my uncle said when she was in college, she was the best actress there. Everyone thought she would end up in Hollywood!

When I told her that Mr. T. had gotten me into the drama class, she was pleased. "Oh, Trisha, you're going to love it. It will bring you out of your shyness. You'll be better than I ever was!" she cooed.

I didn't have the heart to tell her that I hated getting up in front of people and speaking. That when I did, I felt like I couldn't breathe. That I knew I'd fail. All I said was, "I'll never be able to speak in front of people, Mom. Never."

My mother thought for a time then she kissed me.

"Please try, Trish. It will bring a joy to your life that you can't even imagine."

I knew, for once, my mother was wrong.

At first, Mr. Wayne put me in charge of painting the scenery flats for the play—someone had told him I loved art. Most everyone else in the class was working on the play itself. It was called *Musette in the Snow Garden*, about a girl and her friends who disappear from this mysterious garden. Something like a winter Peter Pan. Mr. Wayne had written it. He joked that it was his masterpiece.

After a time I became more and more fascinated listening to the cast rehearse for the play. I found myself mouthing the words as I painted and helped build the sets.

Before long, I knew everyone's part, but no one knew.

Mr. Wayne often invited me to join the rest of the class in exercises. He'd bark an emotion at us and we would immediately show that emotion—fear, anger, curiosity. He had us do word games, too, and had our voices just make noise. ROAWR! HARRUMP! Sometimes he'd tell us all to lie on the floor and put heavy books on our stomachs and make us recite poems. "If these books aren't moving . . . then you aren't using your diaphragms!" he'd say.

I was really beginning to love this class.

One day after I'd been in the class for a few weeks, Mr. Wayne announced who was taking each part in the play. Kathleen Burns would be Musette, the lead. I liked Kathleen, and so did everyone else in school, it seemed. She was a nice person and, what an actress! No wonder Mr. Wayne chose her.

Finally one day as I was finishing up a scenery flap, Mr. Wayne gathered the cast on the stage. "You all should have memorized your parts by now. Remember, on the night of the performance there will be no one but each of you on this stage. You'll have to know your lines by heart!"

"Yes!" they all shouted.

But they didn't. Bobby Ecklund kept forgetting the last part of anything he had to say. Carol Costa spoke so low, who knew if she knew her part. I could see Mr. Wayne growing disappointed.

Then Kathleen Burns, Musette, could hardly remember a single line. "Come to the garden at the winter moon because . . . because . . ."

"Because this is when the magic chair will appear," I blurted out. What was I thinking!

But Mr. Wayne didn't seem to mind, so every time someone forgot a word or a phrase, I shouted it out.

"Patricia!" Mr. Wayne finally said. "Do you know this entire play? By heart?"

I had to think for a moment. "Well, I guess I do," I answered.

"Absolutely splendid!" he said as he smiled. "You must become our prompter."

Yes, I nodded, I could do that—as long as I didn't have to get out on that stage.

Then, just a week before the play, a catastrophe struck! Kathleen Burns's family suddenly moved away. They were just plain gone, without even telling the school.

"What are we going to do?" Carol Costa howled at rehearsal.

"None of us knows her part well enough to step in for her," Donna Biscay said to Mr. Wayne.

"Wait," Kathy Polos called out. "Mr. Wayne, we have Musette. She's been here all along!" She motioned toward me. "Patricia knows every word of the play."

Well, yes, I did. And my mother would be so proud.

But when I looked out into the empty auditorium and tried to say a line, nothing would come out. I felt like I had gulped handfuls of dust and sand.

Finally, all I could manage to get out was a shaky, "No, Mr. Wayne, not me."

Everyone surrounded me. "Patricia, you have to, you just have to," they said.

"Oh, please do it. Please," Mike Conlan added. Mike Conlan had never spoken to me before!

"Well, Patricia, do you think you have it in you to do it?" Mr. Wayne asked.

I just stared at the floor.

"She won't do it," Bobby Ecklund finally scoffed. "She's afraid. She can't even read her English papers out loud in front of the class."

This time Bobby Ecklund was right. I was afraid.

After school that day Mr. Wayne worked with me alone. "Patricia, everyone in class is behind you. All of them will be as nervous as you are to stand up on that stage. Don't you know that? I want you to recite Musette's speech when she is in the garden at midnight." Then he pulled me out to the apron of the stage.

I started to say her lines. I really did know them all by heart, but I looked out at the empty auditorium, and my voice started shaking.

"Say each sentence slowly . . . take a breath between each of them. I notice you're locking your knees. Don't do that. Relax. Move around the stage. You've heard my directions so you know them by heart, too," Mr. Wayne coaxed. "Patricia, let the play take you."

I forgot the audience that wasn't there. I did exactly as he instructed. I let the play take me. With each sentence I seemed to gain a strength I didn't know I had.

"That's it, Patricia. You are my Musette!"

The night of the play, Mom came backstage and helped all of us girls get into our costumes. I was excited, but terrified. I couldn't even remember my opening lines. "How many people will come to see the play?" I asked her. Didn't somebody say it could be over a hundred people? Two hundred?

"It doesn't matter, dear Trish, the moment you step out on stage, everything will come to you."

One hundred people. Two hundred. My heart was pounding really hard and fast. I could hardly breathe.

Carol came up behind me. "You've been perfect in all the rehearsals. You are going to be great!" she whispered.

"But I always rehearsed in front of an empty auditorium," I gulped.

Mr. Wayne heard us. "Remember, my Musette, let the play take you."

Then he brought me up to the stage and we waited in the wings until it was my entrance. I peeked around the curtain. I could see in the darkness the packed audience, mostly adults, but some children. My mouth was dry and I couldn't feel my legs anymore.

I couldn't do this.

But then I heard my cue.

"You're on, Musette," Mr. Wayne whispered and gave me a little push.

I took a deep breath. I unlocked my knees and swayed a little. Musette, I said to myself, and again, Musette. And then I moved out onto the stage.

Without thinking, my first line came out of my mouth. And the second and the third. I moved around center stage to gather my handmaidens, my arms flowing as I called them. I was Musette, and the more I said, the easier it got. The audience disappeared.

I remembered every stage direction that Mr. Wayne had shown me. I gestured. I sang out. I reacted to each of the others. I listened to what they were saying and responded.

Everyone played their roles, too. When Bobby Ecklund flubbed a line to me, he looked lost. But it didn't throw me, I just fed him his next line under my breath.

I was on fire.

The rest of the play went without a hitch. Everyone did a great job, and what I loved most was that I felt like I belonged to something so much bigger than I was. All of us in the play were like family.

And the audience? It stood up and gave us a standing ovation! I couldn't believe it.

After the last curtain call, I found Mr. Wayne. "You were right about everything," I gushed. "Once I started I forgot the audience. No butterflies, no stomachache, no shaky legs. I knew exactly what to say."

"Do you remember that I called my play my masterpiece?"

I said that I did.

"Tonight, Patricia, I have another masterpiece."

"Where is it, Mr. Wayne?" Maybe he'd written another play.

"It's you, Patricia. You showed courage and grace. You stood up to your fears! Tonight, you're my masterpiece."

That magical night has lived in my memory all of these many years. Of course, Mr. Wayne had many many masterpieces. Young people who were just like me. Afraid of stepping on stage, and, like me, afraid to speak in front of anybody. He molded them into miraculous creatures that, because of his workshops and good ideas and his belief in them, discovered the real power they had.

Thanks to him, I did lose my shyness, and I am able to make speeches to crowds of many hundreds. Sometimes thousands. He taught me to speak from the heart and to believe in myself. But most of all he taught me that all of us are masterpieces if given the chance and encouragement—to be one.